THE
DARK GAME

Two Novelettes

DOUGLAS CLEGG

ALKEMARA
PRESS

PUBLICATION CREDITS

Published by Alkemara Press in the United States.

ISBN: 1-944668-12-8
ISBN-13: 978-1-944668-12-9

Books by Douglas Clegg

The Abandoned
Afterlife
The Attraction
Bad Karma
Breeder
The Children's Hour
Dark of the Eye
Dinner with the Cannibal Sisters
Goat Dance
The Halloween Man
The Hour Before Dark
The Infinite
The Lady of Serpents
Lights Out: Collected Stories
Mischief
Mordred, Bastard Son
Mr. Darkness
Neverland
Night Asylum
Night Cage
The Nightmare Chronicles
Nightmare House
The Priest of Blood
The Queen of Wolves
Red Angel
You Come When I Call You

CONTENTS

To Raul

Be sure to visit the author's website at
www.DouglasClegg.com

Subscribe to Douglas Clegg's free email newsletter
at DouglasClegg.com to get book updates, exclusive
excerpts, information on special deals – and more.

The Dark Game

1

I SAW A PAINTING in a gallery once that depicted a man's hands, bound together.

Its title: "Victory is Freedom of Mind and Body."

I believe that is true. I would go further and say that victory is freedom of mind *from* body.

Separation from the thing that imprisons us.

Flight.

Perhaps freedom from life itself.

That is victory.

Life is brutal.

It's like this whip and these ropes. It hurts. It scars. But we must take it.

We must find some pleasure and solace within this terrible lashing.

You want to hear it all? You want me to tell you how it went, in the prison camp? Why I like the ropes?

You want to play the game with me?

First let me tell you this:

Youth is something you put in a drawer somewhere.

You lose the thought of it behind socks and letters and medals and old passport photos and keys that no longer fit locks.

You wear it when you're of the right age, and you do things that you ought not to, and then as you gain perspective with age, you put it away, and you close the drawer.

And you lock it.

Then, you live the life you've built toward, and no one needs to see what's in that drawer.

A secret is something to be hidden.

If is hidden well enough, it never becomes a fact. It is just something that is not there when you go to look for it. It is the thing missing, but the thing that is not missed.

That's how I feel.

That is why I don't revisit those times, often.

The camp.

Or the motel room.

Or the smokehouse.

But since you have me here, like this, I'll tell you.

Maybe you'll leave after that. Maybe you won't want to stay here once you know about me.

2

Before the war, I was in a motel room with a girl I met outside the base.

For fun she tied me up and when she did it, I went someplace else in my head. My hands tied, my feet bound. I remember she smelled like orange blossoms, and she enjoyed tightening the thin ropes around my hands.

But my mind was just gone — drifting upward into darkness, into another place. Back to Burnley Island, I guess, and that's where I've always ended up — *my memories, my family, my home.*

I was just not there anymore. The game had taken me over.

It had become automatic for me.

It was second nature.

In the war, things got worse for me.

The game got worse.

But it wasn't so bad when I was a kid.

3

Early memory:

Winter.

Bitter cold.

Wind whistling around me, boxing my ears, as I trudged through three feet of snow to get out to the smokehouse. I was ten, perhaps. Heavy with a burden.

It was the dog I'd had since he was a foundling of two or three years old, and I was too young to remember bringing him home from a walk in the woods.

He was dying now, of some undiagnosed malady. In those days, you didn't take the dog to the vet when it was its time.

You took him someplace and you shot him.

And this freezing February day, that was what I was to do.

My father marched behind me. I could not bring myself to turn and look over my shoulder to see how he kept pace. I was weeping, and it would be the first and last time I would weep for years.

I held my dog — a small mutt, no bigger than my arms could carry — and he looked up at me as if he understood that something not wonderful was to come.

At the smokehouse I stopped and prayed. I wished that God would intervene, just this once.

I would trade, I promised God, my life for this dog's. I would do anything God wanted me to do if he would just take a minute and breathe new life into my dog's body. I would build a chapel.

No, I would build a *cathedral.*

The snow bit at my cheeks and nose.

My dog, whose name was Mac, whimpered and groaned.

"Go on, son," my father said.

He called me "son" more than he ever used "Gordie" or "Gordon."

Sometimes I thought he wasn't sure of my name. That I was just another son to him. Another child to deal with before I became a man.

I reached up, and opened the door to the smokehouse. I barely kept my balance, for the dog had grown too heavy for me.

My father lit the lantern inside the building —
the smokehouse was old-fashioned, and my
mother felt it was a fire hazard, but my father
insisted on using it.

A yellow flickering light filled the small
room.

After I set Mac down on some straw, I kissed
him on the muzzle and kept my prayers going —
my deals with God to change this, somehow.

Then, my father handed me the pistol and
told me to get it over with quickly.

"Misery is terrible. That animal is in misery.
When you brought him home, you promised to
take care of him. That is a commitment. This is a
way to take care of him, so he won't be in any
more pain. You can stop his pain. He won't get
better, son. He won't."

"I can't," I said.

"You have to. You promised. You promised
me. And you promised that dog when you
brought him home. He has had a good life here.
But now he's sick. And he needs to be taken care
of."

I looked at my dog's face and saw the
terribleness of all existence in his eyes. In his
shivering form.

And that is when I learned about how life doesn't matter at all.

Not one bit.

It is a misery. A wretchedness foisted on us by a God who turns His back on all.

We live on a planet of ice, and the only thing we human beings can do is endure it and try to make sure that we don't add to the misery too much.

4

Here is my life:

I was born on Burnley Island, in a house called Hawthorn, and I grew up in a family called Raglan that had a history on that island.

We were shepherding people, I'm told, originally. We came with Welsh and Scots and English in our blood, and we were dark and swarthy, as I am, a perfect descendant of the Raglan clan.

My father was a brute, and I don't say that lightly. He was a man more likely to lash with a belt or a switch than to scold with words. He was quick to judge, and hot tempered, and I suppose I joined the army to get away from him more than anything else.

I went off to see the world and fight the good fight, and found myself one dawn in the heat of a jungle, in the boredom of a company that was lost, our communications screwed beyond all measure, and I had a "fuck all" attitude toward the war and the jungle.

I was nineteen, and the last place I wanted to be was in that miasma of heat, humidity and the stink of swamp.

And then, before much time had passed, the enemy got us.

No need to go into specifics.

It was ugly.

There were a dozen of us originally, but by the time I regained consciousness, tied like a pig to a stick, there were only eight or so — counting me and my buddy, Gup (short for Guppy, which was a kinder name than his original nickname, which was Shrimp), Davy, who seemed too young to be a soldier, a man I had no liking for (named Larry Pastor), and Stoddard.

I knew what to do if captured — name, rank, serial number, and nothing else.

The truth was, I was scared spitless and we'd all heard the stories of the POWs and how no Geneva Convention was going to stop our enemy from torturing us and then dropping us in some mosquito breeding ground, dead, when it was all over.

None of us was commander.

We were just soldiers, and we had no valuable information at all, and no reason for a negotiation with our commanders.

But hope is the last thing to go, and so we had it.

I had it, and Gup had it, although Stoddard had already told me that he knew he'd die in the jungle and he didn't give a damn because his girl was already pregnant by some other guy and his folks had disowned him for some reason he wouldn't say, and what the fuck was the point?

That was his attitude, and even though I felt we lived on Ice Planet and life was a hurdle into chaos, I still hoped.

For the best. For life. For good to come out of bad.

I woke up later on, pain running through my arms and legs like they'd had nails driven into them. I crouched in a dark hole in the ground that smelled like feces and had just a grate at the top so I could see a little of the sky.

Luckily, I still had a pack of gum on me – I kept it in this small pouch at the back inside of my skivvies that my mother had sewn for me to hide money.

Instead, I hid Wrigley's gum, and I took a sliver of a piece and began chewing it just to feel as if I were still an American and that things mattered even if I was in a hole in the ground.

5

I was a little boy when my mother taught me the game, only it wasn't really a game the way she told me about it. It was a way to get calm and to try and get through pain. I guess I was probably four when she taught me it.

She said my grandmother had taught her, and that her grandfather knew about it, too.

It was like make believe, but when I had scarlet fever as a kid, I really needed something to help me get through it. I was sure I was going to die, even though I didn't know what death was at four.

But scarlet fever gave me an inkling.

I was feverish and delusional, and I remember being wrapped in blankets and taken in the car to Dr. Winding over in Palmerston, and lying naked on his ice cold metal table while his nurse drew out the longest needle I had ever seen in my life and they told me it wouldn't hurt, but I screamed and screamed and my mother and father had to hold me down while that needle went into my butt.

Even though I still had fever, it wasn't quite so bad. But my butt stung, and, wrapped in blankets on the way home, I was in my mother's arms, a baby again. She whispered to me to try the game, that's what she called it.

I named it the Dark Game later on. When it got to me.

At home, in my room, she sat beside my bed and told me to close my eyes despite my moans and groans, and she told me to take her hand. But I couldn't close my eyes. I kept opening them.

Finally she took a handkerchief and put it over my eyes like a blindfold. She began the rhyme. I said it along with her in a singsong kind of voice.

After a bit, she and I were somewhere else, in the woods, in darkness, and I could not feel the pain or the fever at all.

She told me that it was a way the mind worked that was like magic, that it got you out of yourself and out of where you were.

When I began to teach my friends how to do it as a kid, she pulled me aside and told me that I should keep it to myself.

"Why?" I asked.

"Because it can be bad, too. It's important to stay in the world. To not delve into that too much. If you need God, there's church. If you need friends, don't go off into your head too much."

But I didn't understand what she meant then, and I'm not sure I do now.

Or maybe I do and I just don't want to look at it.

"It's a daylight game," she said. "Between you and me. It's a Raglan game. It's just to make things easier when they're rough."

I played it, all by myself, my eyes closed, that wintry day in the smokehouse when I shot my dog, too.

I played it in that hole in the middle of the jungle without a hope in hell of getting out of there alive.

6

The first day and night, They watched me.

'They' being the enemy.

I don't want to call them what we called them back then. It was racist. It was nasty. It was a nasty place to be. I hated their guts.

They were Enemy.

They were *They*.

We were *Us*.

My boys — that's how I thought of Gup and Stoddard and Davy — screamed at night. I heard them clearly. I'm pretty sure Stoddard died right away.

That's what I heard, anyway.

I could picture him working hard to piss off the Enemy, even if his nuts were being nailed to the wall. Gup might hang in there. Davy, I worried most about. He was practically just a kid.

I began to discover my darkness in my dirty pit of a bedroom. I began to feel my environment.

I guess I was about twenty feet down. Some kind of well.

Maybe it had been dug up for water.

Or prisoners. I don't know. It was deep but not wide.

I had just enough room to sit with my knees nearly touching my chest. It was dirt and rock, and they lowered water down after midnight, just a cup on a string. Half the water had dropped out of the cup by the time it reached me.

Not even a cup, I discovered. A turtle shell. Drank out of it because I was damn thirsty, and I soon discovered that if I didn't drink out of it fast, they yanked it back up.

They.

Sons of bitches.

I stared up through the grate, trying to see the stars or at least something that meant the hole was not just an o in the earth that had no beginning and no end.

7

Memory:

Back to Texas, back to the night I got tied up, back when I was barely more than a kid and out on an adventure.

The girl who tied me up was named Genie, and she could be had in that sunbaked Texas town for less than twenty bucks.

I was too young to be sure what I could do with a girl like that — I had left my sheltered island a virgin of eighteen, and knew that I would have six months or so before getting my orders overseas into the heart of the war.

I didn't want to die a virgin; and I doubt there has been a virgin in existence that wanted to die in that state, untouched by another.

So, when my buddies and me went out to the local rat bar called *The Swinging Star*, playing pool and chugging too many beers, I let down my guard a bit when one of my friends, named Harry Hoakes, slapped me on the back and whispered in my ear with his sour mash breath that he and a couple of the guys were going down to Red

Town, a part of the desert where the whores were cheap and fast and you could buy a few for a good deal less than a week's pay.

I look back with shame, of course, upon this youthful episode in my life.

I do not proudly admit that my first experience with a woman was at the hands of a seasoned pro of twenty-six, but it is what it is — or, it was what it was. I was drunk, stupid, pretty sure I was going to die in some distant jungle, so I went with my *compadres* out in a truck that some townie drove — no doubt the pimp for the Red Town girls.

We unloaded outside yet another bar, and went in, and there they were, like glittery fool's gold, or broken glass mistaken for diamonds on a moonlit highway.

Harry Hoakes looked like a movie star and was from L.A. and had this air of magic around him, no matter what he did.

He died in the war, within a year. I heard he stepped on a mine and it just ripped him up.

But that night, he was completely on and alive like lightning — all around you and illuminating the dark.

This landscape was alien to me — slovenly, lazily pretty girls who looked the way whores are supposed to, not quite unhappy yet with their situation, not quite sure of how they landed in that desert canyon, not quite hardened to the way their lives would surely go.

When you're eighteen and in the army, whores don't seem sad or needy or even lesser.

They seem like angels who don't ask for the reasons of your interest. They know you want them, and they're perfectly fine with that.

Harry Hoakes introduced me to the girls like they were his sisters. The one who sidled up to me was Genie.

"I'm like that old movie star, Gene Tierney. From *Laura*. You ever see *Laura*? It's a beautiful movie. I'm gonna be a movie star someday. I *am*."

She was a big brunette with big teeth, from the Midwest, she said, a farm girl who wanted adventure, and intended to wind up in Hollywood in a couple of months — some producer had discovered her already and she was just waiting to hear from him, she told me all of it so fast it made me laugh.

Then, she asked me what I wanted to do.

* * *

17

We got a bottle of Jack Daniels and went back to the motel and plunked down the few bucks for a two-hour stay.

After that, she brought out those ropes from some little overnight bag she lugged around with her.

She told me that since I was a virgin, she wanted to make sure I didn't do any of the work.

That's what she called it, and I guess it was her work.

But when the ropes went on, I went off somewhere.

I was no longer in a rundown motel with a big toothed girl, but back on Burnley Island.

It was winter (as my memories of that New England island often are in a hot, dry, desert place) and my father tied me up to the post that sat at the center of the smokehouse.

He told me I had been bad to do what I had done, and that he had to teach me a lesson.

I was, perhaps, fourteen, my shirt had been torn off my back, and I felt the sting of his cat — a cat-o-nine-tails that he kept to discourage my brothers and me from doing the bad things we often did.

But in my Dark Game memory, I didn't feel pain from the stings — I felt myself glowing, becoming a powerful creature beneath the lashes.

I felt as if I were commanding my father to whip me, to torment me with the bad things I'd been doing. I felt as if I were a god, and he were merely my servant.

And soon, in the Dark Game, it was my father with his shirt torn, tied to the post, and I had the whip, and I was lashing at him and telling him that he was a bad, bad man.

When I opened my eyes, the game done, I found that I was tied to that bed in the motel in Texas. Outside, the sound of trucks going by.

In a corner of the room, Genie, the whore, lay like a crumpled rag doll, her face bloodied.

8

Harry Hoakes came a-knocking at the motel room door. I was tied up in Room 13, which made it lucky, I guess.

He was drunk from his own bottle of Jack Daniels, and he nearly busted down the door to get to me.

Inside, he looked at me, tied up and naked on the dirty bed, and then at Genie, her big teeth all but knocked out, lying in a corner, her eyes wide.

He stared at me, then at her.

"I passed out," I said.

"Jesus H." He scratched his head, dropping his nearly empty bottle. His fly was open from his time with his girl. He was too drunk to process everything. "What the hell?"

"I don't know. I passed out. We didn't even do anything."

"Must've been her pimp," he said.

"She's got a pimp?"

"What, you think she's a nice girl from Iowa?"

"Maybe she's not dead," I said.

"If she's not dead, then she's the greatest actress in the world. Because she's dead like I ever saw dead."

"She thought she was going to be like Gene Tierney."

"Who?"

"That pretty actress with the overbite. In *Laura*. You ever see *Laura*?"

He looked at me kind of funny, and then shook his head. "We are up the legendary creek, my friend. You got a dead whore in your room, and you're...well, naked as a jaybird tied up." Then, he let out a laugh. "Christ, you could not have made this up if you wanted to."

"Help me out of these ropes," I said. "Houdini I ain't."

9

⏤⬥⏤

In the hole, in the prison, the enemy would sometimes stand over the grate and spit.

They did this a lot, and now and then, they'd take a leak down on me. I'd hear *them* laughing up above.

This might've been happened over a few days or a few weeks. I barely saw the sun in that time, because the grate got covered by a board during the day. They didn't want me to get that Vitamin D from the few rays of the sun, I guess.

It was like living in a cave, and time seemed to evaporate.

I lived in endless night.

They'd get me out of there sometimes, too. Usually when it was dark.

They'd send a rope down, and I was to bind my hands to it and they'd pull me up.

Why did I go?

They fed me during those times. Fed me much better than if I stayed in the hole and ignored the rope.

They brought me up and gave me fish or frog or some kind of large maggot cooked with thick flat leaves around it that didn't taste half-bad to a starving guy.

They pretended to be friendly, and the one who spoke English, who I called Harry Hoax after my friend from Texas, because he sounded a little like the real Harry Hoakes, he made light jokes with me about my situation that actually were pretty funny.

So my new friend Hoax took me aside into the mud-brown cell where I'd get the sumptuous feast, and he told me that he was my only friend.

"Your men already betrayed you," Hoax said. "They have told the commander everything. The position of other companies. The plans of the General."

I looked at him, grinning. "I bet they have. Good for them."

"Yes," Hoax said. "It is good. How are you feeling? I see sores on your shoulder."

"I'm fine."

"You seem in good spirits. Are you praying to your god?"

"God has more important things to worry about than me."

"I bet you are thirsty."

"Somewhat."

"Good. We have some pure water for you. And even a small cup of wine. Specially for you."

"To what do I owe this sudden bout of hospitality?"

"We are not primitive people. We may live and fight among the trees and swamps, but we have a sense of culture. You are important to us. We want you happy and healthy."

"That's why you put me in a hole in the ground."

"War is evil. I know that. We know that."

"Am I talking to 'I' or 'We'?"

He laughed.

"Very good. Here," he said, glancing at the doorway.

A young attractive woman entered, a wooden tray in her hands. On the tray, a small porcelain cup, and beside it some palm leaves. Atop the leaves, more of the fried grub I'd had before, and then what looked like a rabbit's leg, also cooked.

After setting this down in front of me, she left and returned moments later with a jug of water.

"You see? We treat you well," Hoax said. "All we ask is that you tell us a few things. They are minor, unimportant questions, really."

"I thought my friends told all. I certainly don't know more than they do," I said.

Suddenly, I heard a wail from one of the other cells.

I tried to place the voice as one of my team, but I could not. I wasn't even sure it was human.

Hoax closed his eyes for a moment as if he didn't enjoy the sound, either. Then, he nodded to the girl with the jug. She rose and poured water into the cup.

I brought the cup to my lips and drank too fast. She refilled the cup; while I sat there with Hoax, she made sure I always had water.

"There is a small bit of opium in the water," he said, softly. "You have pain, and it will help with it."

"You're drugging me?"

He sighed. "I feel bad for the state you're in. It is just a distillation of the poppy. Not enough to make you crave it. Just enough to ease any physical torment you might be feeling."

After a moment, I nodded. "That's kind of you."

"You are different from the others," he said. "You are not like other Americans, Gordon. You have a deeper quality. We do not want to hurt you. We want to bring you into realignment with truth."

"Ah," I said, feeling a bit blurred around the edges. I assumed this was the opium.

Hoax began the routine questioning that had been done before, and I gave him the standard answer, which was no answer at all.

At the end of this, my meal finished, he sighed.

He told me that he wished me no harm but that the war would end with their victory and our defeat and that all my pain would be for nothing.

"Perhaps," I told him. "Or perhaps not."

Two interrogators came in. I recognized in their eyes the sadism I'd seen before. These were pleasure torturers.

I would be their toy for the night.

Hoax left the cell looking a little sad.

The interrogators bound my hands and ankles, and began to play a game that I believe is called, in torturing circles, the Thousand Scratches.

But it didn't matter what they did to my body.

I closed my eyes, and I could begin the rhyme I'd learned as a child:

Oranges and lemons say the bells of St. Clement's.

And then, my mind eroded into darkness: I returned to the smokehouse, tied to the post, with my father's cat-o-nine-tails snapping hard at my scarred shoulders.

10

My father and I had good moments, too.

He took me hunting and fishing. We spent idle summer Sundays out on a skiff that he'd borrowed from a friend down in the harbor, and he told me of his abiding love for the sea.

He took me on his occasional deep sea fishing voyages, and he brought me closer to him when my sister Nora drowned off the island, coming home from the mainland on a small boat when a storm hit.

My father pulled me aside and wept with me, the closest he'd ever come to showing genuine softness and true compassion.

If I felt something other than love for him, it was no doubt honor.

I hated him for the whippings, but I knew that some demon drove him to it. I was willing to take it for the building of my character.

Perhaps these days, people might call the police if a boy were being whipped by his father. But in those times, not long ago, it was considered nobody's business outside of the family's own concern.

My father's demons were many, but he seemed to have an overzealous Christian sense of the Devil and of Angels and of saving his children from the Burning Fires of Hell.

He'd shout at me, while he whipped, that this hurt him more than it hurt me, and that angels and Jesus wept as the lash ripped against my skin but that if I were to go to heaven, I must repent of my sinful ways, of the bad things I had done, and I must turn to Jesus and to God's grace and His iron will.

I was, he told me, of the Devil.

11

Oh, the bad things I'd done, they were truly bad, I suppose.

I smoked a bit, and I drank sometimes when I was far too young to drink liquor.

Once, I tried to set fire to the smokehouse, but only managed to burn most of the field nearby and many of the small thorny trees.

He had also caught me in the woods, in a way that a boy doesn't want to be caught, and that was part of my sin.

I deserved the whippings, and took them, playing the game to get through them, and then would spend a feverish night with my grandmother's salve all over my back to help speed the healing.

I honored and respected my father, even then, and I also thought of ways I might kill him someday.

But I never did.

12

Once I awoke from the game, after the interrogators — my impersonal demons — had left their scratches all over my too-thin body.

They returned me to my pit, to my dark filthy bed.

Sometime later — days, perhaps — I was brought out again.

This time, Hoax was not happy with me. It seemed that my comrades had not said as much as they'd wanted. It seemed that none of us was behaving.

This time, I was to have a night of theater, he told me.

"Might I have a bit of that opium water?" I asked. I might've begged. I liked the stuff and I wanted to make my time in this Hell as pleasant as possible.

"Perhaps after," he said, rather sadly.

I was brought into a cell lit by the wavering flame of a candle.

In a corner, my buddy Davy, *sweet little Davy*.

His eyes, swollen from beatings.

His jaw cracked.

A festering wound on his scrawny arm.

Ropes again. This time, on his wrists and ankles.

Four men held the ends of the rope.

"This is a play we call the Tug of War," Hoax told me.

Then, he began asking me questions.

Tears came to my eyes, but I had nothing to tell them.

The four men tugged at the ropes and I heard Davy's bones pop, one by one, as they pulled, and his jaw dropped open, slack, but he was still alive.

Until one of the men pulled what seemed to be the forearm right out of Davy's skin.

Oh, but the game kicked in again, you see, at that point, and I missed most of the evening's entertainment by flying off to Burnley Island, by going somewhere I would be punished for my sins, but they were *my* sins alone and it was *my* punishment and no one else's.

* * *

When I came out of the game, I was missing a finger and had no memory of it being taken or of the burning metal that had cauterized it to keep it from bleeding.

Hoax, however, told me the next time I was hauled up that I was a man of iron.

"You didn't make a sound. You seemed..."

"To be someplace else," I said.

He nodded. "Where did you go? The one you call Axeman was using a dull small scissor to cut off your finger. Why didn't you flinch?"

"Magic," I told him. "What's on the menu for tonight?"

"Menu?"

"Bugs? Rats? Frogs?"

"Oh," he said, smiling. "Supper. Well, tonight, we have a special treat. Tongue."

"Cow?"

"Pig. But it's very good. Wild pig makes a wonderful dish."

When I was finished with supper — and it truly was sumptuous compared to my previous ones — they brought another from my company, the scrappy little guy we called Gup.

* * *

As with the previous show with Davy, he had obviously been beaten, and perhaps his left leg was broken, also, for he hobbled in and nearly collapsed when the interrogators let go of his arms.

"Your friend cannot speak," Hoax whispered in my ear, like a mosquito circling. "He has, unfortunately, just this afternoon, lost his tongue under the Axeman's blade."

Now, Hoax didn't say that the tongue I had just eaten was my buddy's.

He didn't have to.

Maybe it was, and maybe it wasn't.

But he obviously wanted to give me that message, no matter what the truth of it might be.

I didn't eat for a few days more, but finally, pulled out of the hole again, I gobbled down the food they brought me — a stew made from strips of meat and leaves that tasted terrible but completely satisfied the gnawing in my gut.

Again, Gup was brought out, this time missing both hands, cauterized and bandaged at the wrist.

"His hands fell like leaves from a dying tree," Hoax told me.

"Very poetic," I said, trying to keep my mind from thinking about Gup and the Axeman too much, and forcing myself to keep out of drifting into the Dark Game.

To remain in the moment.

"Have you ever tasted human flesh?" Hoax asked.

I looked at poor Gup's face.

I wished him to die right there. I prayed to God. I prayed to the Devil. I prayed to the Queen of Heaven, Mary, the Mother of God, *Blessed is the Fruit of her Womb, Jesus.*

I prayed that his spirit would be pulled from his body before another night passed.

This entertainment of Hoax's went on for several nights, but each time I refused to answer his questions.

* * *

I will admit with nothing but shame that I began to crave the meals brought to me, and I convinced myself — no doubt for survival's sake — that this was *not* the body of Gup that I slowly consumed, sliced from him day after day and cooked up with spices and aromatic flowers to make dishes that I began to love.

This was simply meat that had been taken from the body of pigs and rats and snakes and lizards and frogs and fish and other creatures of this Enemy's country.

This, a steamy bowl before me, did not hold Gup's foot, sliced into slivers, swimming in fragrant soup.

This was *not* a bit of flayed skin from Gup's buttocks, wrapped within an elephant ear palm leaf that had been buttered and baked into a moist but crunchy crust.

Yet, nightly, Gup was there, before me.

Soon an eye was gone, then his nose, his ears, toes and left foot, his lips sliced off, until I saw him no longer as a man at all, as a friend, as a former buddy, as one of the team.

I saw him as the supplier of my life.

* * *

In a dream, in the hole, I had a vision of the great snake of life, devouring its own tail.

Life eats life, the image of the snake seemed to tell me. Life devours itself. You are part of this, and so is Gup. The snake is the whip in my father's hand. The whip is in my hand and reaches from my bloodied back to whip my father's hand. The torturer and the tortured are each playing a part and cannot be without the other.

I awoke from this dream and knew then that life was neither beautiful nor perfect nor magical.

Life was simply the gutter of heaven, the place where offal and waste stagnated, encircled with pestilence.

* * *

I began to love my suppers with Hoax.

Even when the Axeman came to me, a razor in his hand, and my mind shooting off to the game, I began to enjoy my contact with these cosmic barbarians and I looked forward to whatever they had in store.

I had forgotten my army, my country, and my friends.

There was only my hole and my cell, and my smokehouse back on my beloved home island.

It was the whole universe, and I could not tell whether it was heaven or hell.

Then, coming from the Dark Game out into the cell again, it was pain in my crotch that had me screaming, yet I felt distant from the scream.

I felt I could measure the scream and how it flew along the cell walls, bouncing up and down and back again.

They took another one of my fingers, but worse, one of my nuts was felled that night.

The Axeman had done it with his little razor.

I hadn't answered the questions and they had taken my left ball after slicing off my next finger down from my already-torn-off pinkie.

When I came around, I was in the cell, screaming, and one of my guys — Larry Pastor — sat across from me, watching me, his face trembling as if with an impending storm of sobs.

I had become the new entertainment for someone else now.

I was the star of the show.

* * *

The next night, I had the best supper yet, with Larry staring at me from across the room, his face a grimace.

What was I eating? My finger? My testicle? Or simply some special sliced rat over a bed of eel-leaves?

"It's all right," I told him. "It tastes good. It really does."

13

I wasn't sure what I ate most nights, but the strangest thing of all was that I had begun gaining weight.

I still drank a bit of the opium water — Hoax would bring in barely a thimbleful. I guess he wanted to keep me pliable yet sober enough when necessary.

I attributed my gain in bulk to a combination of the fatty meat they fed me, as well as sitting in a hole in the ground for days on end.

Hoax commented on my healthy look and I could see it in Larry Pastor's eyes — while he got thinner and thinner, no doubt refusing to eat any meat offered him, I was beginning to pack on the pounds.

Truth was, I felt better.

I felt as if my mind had adjusted to the hole and the cell.

I began to realize that, contrary to what Hoax might've thought, I never even felt I was going to escape. I just refused to tell Hoax or his beloved Axeman any military plans or secrets because I knew that once I told, I was as good as dead.

The meals would stop.

They'd leave me in the hole and either forget about me completely, or fill it in with dirt and rocks.

I began to see my imprisonment as a kind of luxury hotel — a fancy five-star place.

I began living in my head a lot, believing that I went on adventures when I was in the hole. I used the Dark Game to get out — I began to see the world again.

I was in Paris, briefly, for a moonlit walk along the Seine with a beautiful girl who reminded me of a teacher I'd once had a crush on.

I ate a delicious breakfast on the Champs-Élysées, buttered almond croissant and a demitasse of espresso while watching traffic as it headed toward the Arc de Triomphe.

Another voyage out, I sat upon a striped blanket along the beach of some tropical island, surrounded by bare breasted beauties. I feasted on juicy mango and velvet coconut milk, feeling warm breezes as the shadows of palm trees cast thin lines along the pumice-strewn sand.

In the cell, I'd go to Burnley Island, to a moment in the past; but in the hole, I'd be somewhere magnificent, off on some adventure that was like a wish fulfillment of my boyhood.

Perhaps this saved me.

Perhaps it damned me.

In my rare moments of lucidity, I'd try to stay grounded by chewing on a small bit of the

Wrigley's gum — the little I had left. A tiny infinitesimal piece. It reminded me of who I was, where I was, why I was there.

I began to talk to Hoax, without even knowing that I might be giving away secrets.

* * *

I told him all kinds of things. Not military secrets. Just about my life.

About my nocturnal adventures.

Hoax became my best friend, and I suppose months passed.

Other soldiers were captured. Sometimes I saw their faces, and now and then I recognized them.

But they were part of the *Show* now. I watched the Show, or they watched me in their version of the Show.

But Hoax didn't let the Axeman cut from me again.

My performances for the horror of the new recruits tended to be drawn from the contortionist's trade. My limbs were pummeled and pulled and twisted.

I felt none of it, off in my game.

I was valuable. I began telling things here and there. Nothing important, of course, but I'd become quite a good storyteller as I gained weight from my substantial meals.

My tales of wonder and awe for my host, the polite Mr. Hoax, were about life outside of the jungle, and he loved these adventures into other worlds. He had studied the works of Shakespeare, so now and then we'd talk about *Macbeth* or about *Othello*, and I told him about *Moby Dick* and how my island was somewhat like Nantucket and had been part of the whaling trade.

He loved American movies, too, so we talked about them at some length, and he offered up critiques that were quite well-thought-out about how Americans approached movies as opposed to other cultures. He also enjoyed discussing famous wars, and warriors of the ancient world.

These conversations often went on during the torture of another countryman of mine, usually roughly my age, once handsome, once with dreams and a sense of goodness of the world, all of them still having some meat on their bones.

I watched a man weep as the Axeman sliced off both of his ears, and then held them high for me as if ready to toss them to a trained seal.

I am ashamed to admit that, deluded and not really as sane as I should've been, I clapped for this performance because I thought it was some kind of special effects magic.

The Axeman was good at his job.

I had no idea what Hoax had in store for me, but soon enough, he brought me into a lower level of Hell with him.

14

Here's the thing about the Dark Game:

By itself, it's simply a mind trick. It's a way to open doors inside you and to escape. Pain. Hurt. Sorrow.

That's all it is.

But in that prison camp, with the techniques they taught purely by trying them on me, I learned how to add another level to the game.

How to make it go deeper.

And when it did, something truly magnificent came of it.

15

———◇•◇———

"Brainwashing."

It sounds like some medical experiment.

But it's really simple.

You just put the subject in a position of separation from every sensory detail.

And then you go to work on him.

I had been prepared for it, in my training.

But I guess you're never really prepared for this kind of thing, not after months in a hole in the ground, not after watching your friends get their noses and eyes and ears and hands cut off in front of you.

Not after they feed you what might be your left ball.

16

———◇•◇———

Hoax had me bound up, hands in front of me, but tied to another rope that went to my ankles.

They positioned me, standing, in the middle of a cell.

Plugged a fan into the wall. I guessed this was to help block out any noise beyond the cell wall.

Then, each wall was covered with a dark cloth to block out even the cracks of light that might come in.

Additionally, Hoax tied a blindfold around my eyes.

Plunged into absolute darkness, I felt Hoax touch my hands.

"You are going to be here for several hours," he said. "You are not going to touch the wall. Or sit down. Or fall. Should you fall, you will be strung up so that you are dangling from the ceiling with a stick thrust between your arms to keep you balanced.

"So, do not fall, that is my advice, my friend. You are to keep silent. If you cannot keep silent, our mutual friend Axeman will cut out your tongue and sew your lips together. Understood?

"This is for your betterment. We find that you are truly a patriot to the world, to freedom, and to honor. We want you to realign yourself with nature and man's true calling, instead of with this monster you have served in America. You have been deluded by your country, and we intend to help you recover. You are special to us, and to me, Gordon. You are worth realigning. I consider you my friend."

These were the last words I heard for many hours, during which my bones ached, my bowels let loose without my being able to control them.

After awhile, I felt as if I were floating.

The sound of the fan — a buzzing like a thousand black flies — seemed to take over my mind, as if it were what my brain generated: the noise of a cosmic buzzing.

Somewhere beneath it, after awhile, I heard Hoax's voice again, only I could not make out what he was saying.

I was fairly certain, however, that he existed inside my head, washing my brains the way he might wash his hands with a feminine delicacy, planting ideas and truths known only to the Enemy, trying to make me over into one of his house servants.

I went into the Dark Game. I heard Hoax clearly inside the game itself. I understood how this brainwashing could serve the Dark Game — and how it could help me survive.

* * *

Getting into your brain isn't the problem with brainwashing. Anyone with a good mental crowbar can unlock that mush of gray matter.

It's making your mind separate from your body so completely that your body becomes a servant to someone else's mind.

That is the goal of brainwashing.

They are not cleansing the brain. They are turning it off, and switching on another brain, imprinting another set of memories and values and thoughts so that your past is no longer there.

It is wiped out, but not so completely – you think you are the same person. But someone else has invaded you.

The Other. The one who has turned off one switch has juiced you from another one.

And you are that person's mind now. You are that person's imagination.

That is what I learned. That is how I began to understand that the Dark Game was not just for one to go off on flights of fancy. To protect you from some pain of life.

It could be changed, using this brainwashing.

It could become a way to turn a switch in another — to implant your own mind into another's mind, so that he no longer had his own perception but might, at least briefly, have yours.

I knew there was a way I could use this on Hoax.

On the Axeman.

I knew that there was a way I could put the Dark Game into them so that I might escape.

17

They told me later that I stood there for twenty hours.

They told me later that I had been realigned.

But I had not been.

The Dark Game had saved me. It had protected me. It had kept me from letting their words and thoughts press into my gray matter.

When they brought me out into the sunlight — for the first time in many months — they rejoiced and called me *Comrade* and *Friend* and *Healed One.*

But, on the inside, I had already begun planning how I would destroy them, set their camp on fire, and sow the ashes with salt so that those demons might never rise again.

18

But I've got to pull you back to that night when I was young and in a bad part of some Texas town.

Remember?

Me, tied to the bed, the dead whore on the floor and the real Harry Hoakes, my buddy, my pal, untying me, his breath all whiskey and perfume absorbed from his girl for the night.

"She thought she was going to be like Gene Tierney," I said, and then, "Jesus, I'm going to end up in jail for this."

"Or you'll be in the jungle. In the goddamned war. Which do you want?"

"I choose the goddamned war."

Harry grinned, slightly, despite everything. "You didn't do it. You were tied up. I'm a witness to that."

I got up and got dressed as fast as I could, tripping over my trousers as I yanked them up.

"You let her tie you up?" He laughed.

I shot him a glance that shut him up.

"What are we going to do?" He said.

"We ain't gonna get caught, that's for damn sure," I said.

Next thing I remember, we're dragging that body out to Harry's car, and we plop her in the trunk.

I looked at her once, in that fizzling little light of the trunk, before we shut it down on her.

Her face.

She was somewhere else.

That's what Death is, I thought. It's going into the Dark Game for good.

I had no feeling for her. She was no longer there.

But the drive out to the mesa, thirty miles away from Red Town, the whole way I kept wondering how she had been murdered, and why I woke up from the Dark Game with the strange feeling of pleasure in my loins as if I had truly lost my virginity that night.

But that remains a Mystery with a capital M.

Part of me has felt all these years that I had untied myself, had beaten her to death, and then had somehow wrapped myself up in the ropes again.

Houdini, after all.

* * *

We buried her in a desolate spot, so deep that the coyotes and scavengers wouldn't be able to dig her up.

I heard, years later, that Red Town eventually flourished and became more than a saloon and whorehouse railroad stop. It expanded out into the mesa.

I think that at some point a shopping mall was built near that grave of the girl who thought she looked like Gene Tierney and kept a rope in her overnight bag.

* * *

Harry said to me, at four that morning, driving back to base, "No matter what happens, we can't ever say we met her. Or were even there. The other girls won't tell. They don't like cops. But you and I have to be clear on this. We were never there."

"Where?" I asked, and then Harry muttered, "Jesus," and I knew our friendship was over that morning.

When I heard he died later, in the war, I felt bad for him. I missed him, too. We had done our time together, and that's a bond that remains even after death.

I wonder if he ever got over the sight that had greeted him when he stepped out of the ordinary world of red light night and into that motel room of me tied up and a dead woman on the floor.

But now, he's in the Dark Game.

19

Suddenly, like an overnight celebrity, I became revered among the Enemy in our camp.

No longer made to sleep in the hole, I had a straw mattress beneath me, and I ate regular food with some of the lower officers.

More of my own countrymen arrived at the camp. I observed them as they trooped in, proud and wounded. Some of them spat at the ground as they marched by me.

* * *

The camp spread across a flat wetland area with long planks laid across muddy ground, rising to low hills where most of the buildings sat, and behind which on a kind of plateau, dotted with the holding wells for prisoners.

The commander's headquarters sat at the highest point of one of the hills, and I got to calling it Mount Olympus. The pits and holes where the Americans were kept, I called Tartarus.

I taught Hoax about the various levels of Hell, and he and I cooked up a scheme to begin a new set of torments for my countrymen.

* * *

We would take *Dante's Inferno*, which was easy enough to find even with the supposed anti-European sentiment of the Enemy and from it create elaborate Rings of Hell for the prisoners.

Next, I talked about the cannibal torture. I suggested a whole new way to do this.

Why even use the Axeman? For despite his pleasure in the art of cutting flesh and bone from a live victim, wouldn't there be a more effective Host of such theatrics?

Why not *me*, their countryman?

What would be more horrifying than a well-fed compatriot slicing off the lips of his fellow American in front of the remnants of a once-proud platoon?

A USO show from Hell, I called it. We'll make it a grand show, a hot ticket in the hot jungle. A feast for the eyes and ears. We'd entertain Hoax's soldiers, as well as mesmerize my American friends.

It took Hoax several days to see this as the grandiose and intriguing idea that it might be.

But then he smiled and nodded. "Yes, my friend Gordon, this might be quite a wonderful and acceptable entertainment."

The USO Show from Hell would begin.

* * *

We'd have beautiful girls dancing for the boys.

Then, we'd have the main event. I'd do a comedy routine, I told Hoax.

I'd strip them of their dignity. I'd cut off bits and pieces of the happiest, sweetest guy they knew, the youngest of their friends, the ones they thought of as mascots and baby brothers.

Right before their eyes.

"They'll tell you what you want to know," I said. "They'll divulge their mother and father's addresses if you want, once we do this."

Hoax, not suspicious in the least, was thrilled.

Yet, he still didn't completely trust me, for he felt the Axeman should be there to do the slicing.

I wasn't to be handed knives or razors. I was still a prisoner, albeit a *Friend of Our Country*, as they proclaimed loudly, nightly, into the pits and holes of Tartarus, making sure that every single captured American soldier knew my name and where I'd been born and what I'd done for my newly adopted fatherland.

Once everything was set, the prisoners began building the stadium.

20

I oversaw its construction, and they worked tirelessly and swiftly, for I told them that it was a monument to their Dead.

That it was their Memorial and that they must take pride in it.

I spent some nights with them, talking of how we were going to be well-treated by our captors, and that they must trust me, despite appearances.

They didn't trust me at all, I could tell, but they had the resignation of those who wait for freedom to come from outside their sphere. The helicopter raids from the sky, perhaps, they hoped. The end of the war itself was not too much to wish for in their current state.

They had lost all will to escape. They were broken, yet capable men.

They did as I told them to do.

I also spent nights with them, playing the Dark Game.

I needed their minds. I need to bring them into a state of calm and of service.

I needed for them to hear only *my* voice among all the voices of their prison.

The bleachers went up, the theater backdrop created.

21

Within two weeks, it was, by the standards of the jungle, a beautiful imitation of an amphitheater, and could seat forty or fifty men.

The night of what I called *The Most Magnificent Show in the Universe*, finally arrived.

A banner announcing this, painted from human blood, hung from the wall.

* * *

The celebrities of our Damnation were there: the Commander, with his long face and inscrutable gaze; my friend Hoax, a chubby, round-faced fellow who whispered in the Commander's ear, no doubt about the show to come; the Enemy soldiers, dressed as if for an evening at the theater.

No doubt the women with some of them were not wives, but girlfriends who lived in the nearby Enemy Town, just beyond our Doom City.

The girls had fine red or blue dresses on, as if they would go to a celebration after the show. The men were dressed in full military garb. Cocktails were served, a rarity at this outpost, but the liquor had been distilled from a local flower, and left behind a scent in the air like jasmine.

The atmosphere fairly crackled with the electric moment to come.

I felt as if we were going to stage a great Broadway show. Or a spectacular Fourth of July fireworks demonstration.

It would be, I was certain, the inauguration of some wonderful event that might be remembered and talked about for years to come.

Was I nervous? Of course. How could I pull off such a scheme? What if I were found out? What if something went wrong? If one thing had gone wrong, one tiny thing, all of it would fall like dominoes and it would make stepping on a mine seem like a walk in the park.

* * *

The usual excitement of opening night spread, even among my countrymen. They were brought in, roped at the hands, shackled at the legs, shuffling to their seats, although I kept a contingent backstage, those American actors in the drama to unfold.

Footlights consisted of small fatty candles laid in a semi-circle around the stage floor.

The backdrop, an enormous canvas that had once been an officer's tent covering but was now painted with scenes of the Enemy's Great Leader, stepping on all symbols of the USA. There was a ragged Statue of Liberty crumbling, there Uncle Sam, blinded and toothless his top hat a wreck, and there along the edges was our president being corn-holed by one of our great generals.

Just seeing the backdrop made the Enemy guard cheer and raise their glasses.

What they didn't know, of course, was that I had made sure that a quite a bit of the opium water that I had grown to know well was stirred into their drinks.

I led them in their national anthem. They stood and sang bravely and happily, they drank — all, including the girls — I could tell from their expressions that they had begun to go into a blurred state — the strong alcohol and the poppy milk made themselves known.

As the crowd quieted, and the lights came up, I announced from my perch at the edge of the stage:

"We are gathered here for a momentous occasion! This is the inauguration of a great moment of historical significance!

"We are all the proud and the brave who have learned so much from our new masters, our friends and who wish to teach us the error of our ways and the true path of life! Here, on this very stage, you will see the wonders of transformation!

"You will see the magic of the ancients! The famous tricks of the fakirs of India! The secrets of the alchemists of old Europe! The mystical wonders of the sorcerers of ancient Mesopotamia!"

I spouted all the bullshit I could, and Hoax stood up and translated every word for the Enemy. They laughed, and brawled while some of my countrymen portrayed the President and our military leaders. They tripped, simulating intercourse with each other, acting like buffoons and idiots, all at my command.

The laughter from the stadium was enormous, even from Americans, whom I had brought into a state of the Dark Game just for this evening.

Hoax probably laughed the hardest, and once, when I glanced up at him, I saw the Enemy Commander slap him on the shoulder and whisper some approval in his ear that made Hoax beam.

The dancing girls came out next — they writhed and gyrated for the men. I had given them unhealthy doses of the local drink, and they began touching each other and taking off their clothes until they were nearly naked. This got the Enemy to cheer further, and the girls threw garments up to them.

My own countrymen sat quietly, as I had commanded for them to do in the Dark Game.

I could see that their eyes were glazed over, and they awaited my word.

Finally, to the delight of all, I announced the evening's entertainments.

"Tonight, good gentlemen and ladies, for your pleasure, the Axeman and I will carve up several Americans before your eyes. They will devour one another, as that is the way of our kind, and you will see how corrupt in our very beings we truly are. But first, I ask for volunteers from among you. For I want you to participate greatly tonight. Do I have any takers?"

The Enemy ranks roared approval, and many leapt from their seats to volunteer. But I wanted a special man to come forward. I wanted an important man.

"Commander!" I called out.

"Yes!" cried my countrymen, "Commander!"

Hoax laughed, clapping his hands, turning to his leader.

"Commander!" he said.

The Commander shook his head violently, laughing the entire time.

While he resisted coming forward, I brought the few remaining men from my own company out on the stage. They were further along in the Dark Game than the other prisoners.

Each was blindfolded, and they held each other's hands. I had spent four nights with the three of them to make sure that their minds were switched into another realm, so that my voice and my mind was their only guide.

"Commander!" I cried out again, and even the Axeman, coming up beside me, raised his glinting blade as it caught the last of the sunlight and called the Commander by full name.

Finally, goaded, blurred from drink, the Commander came down from the bleachers.

I raised a hand and called out a word of cheer, and all the Americans began clapping for him, and soon the guards clapped as well, whistling, as their beloved leader stepped up on stage.

"We have a magic show tonight!" I shouted to the noisy audience. "But we must have silence, now! Absolute silence!"

Within a minute or two, those in the bleachers quieted.

I glanced up at Hoax who smiled and nodded as if watching his prize protégé.

I thought of my friend Harry, blown to bits by a landmine. I thought of little Davy, tortured in front of me, tortured until his last breath left him.

I crouched down at the edge of the stage and blew out more than half the candles.

The sun had begun its descent and a gradually-creeping darkness seeped in like a dreadful mist.

Only six or so candles remained flickering, providing scant illumination to our stage. It was an effect I'd worked on — the backdrop now seemed ominous and evil — the Commander's face on the backdrop seemed to have gone in shades into a diseased, corrupt form rather than the healthy look that backdrop had when sunlight was upon it.

The crowd quieted even further, although I heard murmurs among the Enemy that set my teeth on edge.

They had begun to feel uneasy.

* * *

The Commander stepped up next to me, and patted me on the shoulder.

He announced to the crowd that I was a shining example of the realignment procedure that had been developed in the Great City.

I told the Axeman that it was time to begin the carving of the Americans.

He brought the blade up to the ear of one of my boys.

I stopped him, and announced, "Why an ear? Can you make a good purse from it, ladies?"

A tittering came from the women in the bleachers as if this were the cutest of jokes.

"I think not! Why not flay him alive? Right now? But even better, see how his friends," I pointed to the other two men, "don't know what's to come? Their ears are stuffed with wax. Their eyes are covered! Why not have them skin their friend for the delight of the Commander?"

Cheers went up, as I had expected.

In the dark, of course, it was the Americans who began the cheer, but in a stadium, cheers and claps become contagious. People want to be enthused about a show, and so the Enemy began crying out for more.

Then, when they quieted, I asked the Axeman for his blade.

Now, this was the point when my nerves nearly destroyed what I was about to do.

What if?

I felt sweat break out along my back. If he didn't pass me that weapon, none of this would work. If the drinks and the crowd didn't work on him, if he suspected anything...

The Axeman gave me a strange look, but his commander, the Supreme Leader of the camp, nodded to him, and shouted in their language.

The pressure of an audience watching did exactly what I wanted it to do – the Commander was caught up in the magic of the theatrical moment. He wanted the show to go on as planned.

Reluctantly, the Axeman passed me the blade.

It was heavy, and its edge was sharp.

"You will now see," I announced, "one of the Corrupt Americans be skinned before you, and before your Commander, by his own compatriots!"

The audience went silent as I passed the blade to one of my blindfolded men.

Quickly, however, I took it back, and whispered to the three men whose ears were not, in fact, blocked, "Now. To your left."

I turned with the blade, and stabbed the Axeman in the groin, and then cut my way up into his belly and sternum —

As the audience began to gasp —

The three men, blindfolded, grabbed the Commander and tore at him as if they were wild dogs.

In their heads, they were wolves, in fact, and they believed that they were tearing at a stag in the hunt.

The commander screeched, but the men were strong, and in the darkness of the stadium, the Enemy rose, panicking, but it was too late.

They had drunk the opium and liquor, and my countrymen had already risen up with gnashing teeth and a strength that they had never known they'd had in their bodies.

I wanted to see Hoax one last time, to see the look on his face when he knew that this had not gone his way. That he had misplaced any trust he had in me.

But I couldn't find his face in the confusion.

I heard what sounded like wolves tearing at bleating sheep in the dark.

22

The beauty of the escape of my men — men from various platoons who now thought of me as their hero — was that none could remember the show at all.

By dawn, not all the prisoners had survived. Many had died in the fight.

But those who lived, blood on their faces and blotching their clothes, awoke without memory of the past year.

They didn't know the atrocity committed against them, neither did they know of their own savagery, which had killed the Enemy in the camp.

By dawn, I commanded the men, still under the influence of the Dark Game, to set fire to the last of Hell.

23

---◆---

An old memory: I was sixteen, and my father lay dying in his bed.

My mother, who had to take up work now, needed me home to help nurse him while he was in pain.

I sat each day with him, and one morning, when I brought his breakfast, which he barely touched, he told me, "You're an evil son-of-a-bitch, Gordie. You show the world how good you are, but I know who you are on the inside. I've seen it since you were a baby. You have the Devil in you, and you spend your time hiding it."

I sat with him, patiently, nodding so that I might not appear to be the bad child.

Then, when he was through talking about my evil and how I was going to Hell, I offered him a glass of water.

He drank it, greedily, and passed the glass back to me.

"I still love you, dad," I said.

"I know you do," he said.

In the afternoon, he died, peacefully, in his sleep.

I missed him terribly.

His lifeless body, in that bed, made me remember the day he had me shoot my dog and had taught me about how sometimes, Death could be a friend.

24

There. I've told you it all.

I've told you about the war, and the young woman, and my father.

My youth, pulled from the drawer, so you can look at it and judge me.

I should be tied up.

Bound.

Whipped.

It is the only way for me to go out of this body, the freedom of my mind to wander.

It intensifies the Dark Game for me.

I don't want to remember anymore.

I want to close the drawer now.

I want to lock up the past.

I give to you, my wife, Mia, the key.

I Am Infinite,

I Contain Multitudes

1

FIRST OFF, I'LL TELL YOU, I got a peek at both their files. Joe's *and* the old man's.

I bribed a needy psych tech with all kinds of unpleasant favors, but I got my grubby mitts on those folders.

Here's what I found out about Joe:

He had murdered, sure, but more than that, he had told his psychiatrist that he wanted only to help people.

He just wanted to keep them, all these lost souls, from hurting themselves.

He wanted to *love*.

Remember this.

It makes sense of everything I've been going through at Aurora.

I found out things about the old man, as well, but it was all too late by then, wasn't it?

* * *

Let me tell you something about Aurora, something that nobody seems to know but me:

It is forsaken. Not just because of what you did to get there, or how haywire your brain is, but because it's built over the old Aurora.

Right underneath it, where we do the farming. I heard this from Steve Parkinson, right underneath it is the old Aurora.

I saw pictures in an album they keep in Intake.

It used to be a dusty wasteland.

Yes, the old, ancient Aurora once existed smack dab underground. Back then they believed it was better, if you were like us, to never see the light of day, to be chained like animals and have your food shoved to you in a slot at the bottom of your door.

Back then, they believed that nobody in the town outside the fence wanted to know that you were there. But that's not why it's forsaken.

You will know soon enough.

There was a town of Aurora once, too, but then it was bought out by Fort Salton, and 'round about 1949 they did the first tests.

I heard, from local legend, that there were fourteen men down there, just like in a bunker at the end of the war.

They did the tests out at the mountain, but some people said that those men in Aurora, underground, got worse afterward.

I heard a story from my bunkmate that one guy got zapped and fried right in front of an old-timer's eyes. Like he was locked in on the wrong side of the microwave door.

The old-timer, he's still at Aurora; been there since he was nineteen, in 'forty-six. Had a problem, they said, with people after the war.

He was in the Pacific, and had come back more than shell-shocked.

That's all I ever knew about him, before I arrived. You can safely assume that he killed somebody or tried to kill himself or can't live without wanting to kill somebody.

It's why we're all here.

He's about as old as my father, but he doesn't look it. Maybe Aurora's kept him young.

He was always over there, across the Yard. He knew everything about everyone. I knew something about him, too. Actually, we all pretty much knew it.

He thought he was Father to us all. I don't mean like my father, or the guy who knocked your mother up. I mean the Father, as in God The.

In his mind, he created the very earth upon which we stood, his men, his sons.

He could name each worm, each sowbug, each and every centipede that burrowed beneath the flagstone walk; the building was built of steel and concrete and had been erected upon the backs of laborers who had died within the walls of Aurora; the sky was anemic, the air dry and calm; he could glance in any direction at any given moment and know the inner workings of his men as we wandered the Yard, or know, in a heartbeat, no, the whisper of a heartbeat, where our next step would take us.

There was no magic or deception to his knowledge.

He was simply aware; call it, as he did, hyperawareness, from which had come his nickname, Hype.

He was also criminally insane by a ruling of the courts of the state of California, as were most men in Aurora.

I watched him sometimes, standing there while we had our recreation time, or sitting upon the stoop to the infirmary, gazing across the sea of men.

His army, he called them, his infantry: they would one day spread across the land like the fires of Armageddon.

The week after Danny Boy got out was the first time he ever spoke to me.

2

"Hey," Hype called out, waving his hand. "Come on over here."

I glanced around. *Me?*

I had been at Aurora for only four months, and I'd heard the legends of Hype. How he called on you only after watching you for years. How he could be silent for a year and then, in the span of a week, talk your head off.

I couldn't believe he was speaking to me. He nodded when he saw my confusion. I went over to him.

"You're the one," he said, patting me on the back.

You couldn't help but look him in the eye, he was so magnetic, but all the guys had told me *not* to look him in the eye, not to stare straight at him at any point. They all warned me because they had failed at it. They had all been drawn to his presence at one time or another.

He was pale white. He kept in the shack at all times. His hair was splotchy gray and white and longer than regulation. His eyes were nothing special: round and brown and maybe a little flecked with gold. ("He milks you with those eyes," Joe had told me.) There were wrinkles on his face, just like with any old man, but his were thin and straight, as if he had not ever changed his expression since he'd been young.

"*I'm* the one? The *one*," I said, nodding as if I understood.

I had a cigarette, left over from the previous week. I offered it to him.

He took the cigarette, thrust it between his lips, and sucked on it.

I glanced around for an orderly or psych tech, but we were alone together. I didn't know how I was going to light the cigarette for him. They all called me Doer, which was short for Good-Doer, because I tended to light cigarettes when I could, shine shoes for one of the supervisors I'd ass-kiss, or sweep floors for the lady janitors.

I did the good deeds because I'd always done them, all my life. Even when I murdered, I was respectful. But since there was no staff member around, I couldn't get a light for the old man.

Hype seemed content just to suck that cigarette, speaking through the side of his mouth.

"Yeah, you know what it means, but you're it. Danny Boy, he would've been it, but he had to pretend."

He drew the cigarette from his mouth and held it in his fingertips, "He is of a certain breed of sociopath, you must've recognized that. He had to perform for his doctor and the board. He studied Mitch over in B—the one who cries and moans all the time. Mitch with the tattoos?"

I nodded.

"He studied him for three years before perfecting his technique. Let me tell you about Danny Boy. He was born in Barstow, which may just doom a man from the start. He began his career by murdering a classmate in second grade. It was a simple thing to do, for they played out in the desert often, and it was not unusual for children to go missing out there. He managed to get that murder blamed on a local sad little man.

"Later, dropping out of high school, he murdered a teacher, and then, when he killed three women in Laguna, he got caught.

"The boy could not cry. It was not in him to understand why anyone made a fuss at all over murder. It was as natural to him as is breathing to you."

Hype paused, and drew something from his breast pocket.

He flicked his lighter up and lit the cigarette. Although we weren't supposed to have lighters, it didn't surprise me too much that Hype managed to keep one. As an old-timer he had special privileges, and as something of a seer, he was respected by the staff as well as by his men.

It's strange to think that I was suitably impressed by this, his having a lighter, but I was. It might as well have been a gold brick, or a gun.

He continued:

"Danny Boy is going to move in with one of the women who work in the cafeteria. She's never had a lover, and certainly never dreamed of having one as handsome as Danny Boy. Within six weeks, he will kill her and keep her skin for a souvenir. Danny Boy would've been it, but he wasn't a genuine person. You are. You know that, don't you?"

"What, I 'cry,' so that makes me real?"

He shook his head, puffing away, trying to suppress a laugh.

"No. But I know about you, kid. You shouldn't even be here, only you come from a rich family who bought the best lawyer in L.A. I assume that in Court Ninety, he argued for your insanity and you played along 'cause you thought it would go easier for you in Aurora or Atascadero instead of over in Chino or Chuckawalla. Tell me I'm wrong. No? How long you been here?"

"If you're so smart, you already know."

"Sixteen weeks already." He grinned, shaking his head. "Sixteen weeks of waking up in a cold sweat with Joe leaning over your bed. Sixteen weeks of playing baseball with men who would be happy to bash in your head just for the pleasure of it. Sixteen weeks hearing the screams, knowing about Cap and Eddie, knowing about how all they want is the taste of human flesh one more time before they die. And you, in their midst."

He seemed to be enjoying his own speech.

"You're not a sociopath, son, oh no, you're just someone who happened to kill some people and now you wish you hadn't, and maybe you wished you were in Chino getting bludgeoned and raped at night, but at least not having to deal with this zoo."

The bell rang.

I saw Trish, the rec counselor, wave to us from over at the baseball diamond. She was pretty, and we all wanted her and we were all protective of her, too, even down to the last sociopath.

"Looks like it's time for phys ed," Hype said. "She's a fine piece of work, that one. Women are good for men. Don't you think? Men can be good, too, sometimes, I guess. You'd know about that, I suppose."

"What am I 'it' for?" I asked, ignoring the implication of his comment.

He dropped the cigarette in the dust. "You're the one who's getting out."

3

In the late afternoon, I sat beside Joe on the leather chairs in the TV room after we got shrunk by our shrinks.

I said, "I don't get it. If Danny Boy wasn't it, and 'it' means you get out, why the hell am I it?"

Joe shrugged. "Maybe he means 'you're next.' That old guy knows a shitload. He's God."

Joe had spent his life in the system.

First, at Juvy, then at Boys' Camp in Chino, then Chino, and finally some judge figured out that you don't systematically kill everyone from your old neighborhood unless you're not quite right in the head. But Joe was a good egg behind the Aurora fence.

He needed the system and the walls and the three hots and a cot just to stay on track.

Maybe if he'd been in some strict religion or in the army, with all those rules, he never would've murdered anybody. He needed rules badly, and Aurora had plenty for him. He had always been gentle and decent with me, and was possibly my only friend at Aurora.

I nudged him with my elbow. "Why would I be it?"

"Maybe he's gonna break you out," Joe whispered, checking the old lady at the desk to make sure she couldn't hear him. "He broke another guy out awhile back, through the underground. That old man's got a way to do it, if you go down in that rat nest far enough. I heard."

Joe grabbed my hand in his, clutching it, his face inches from mine. "He knows where the way out is, and he only tells it if he thinks your destiny's aligned with the universe."

I almost laughed at Joe's seriousness. I drew back from him. "You got to be kidding."

Joe blinked.

He didn't like being made fun of.

"Believe what you want. All's I know is the old man thinks you're *it*. Can't argue with that."

And then Joe kissed me gently, as he always did, or tried to do, when no one was looking, and I responded in kind.

It was the closest thing to human warmth we had in that place.

I pulled away from him when a psych tech strolled in with one of the shrinks.

Ч

I wanted to believe that Hype could break me out of Aurora. I

I spent the rest of the day and most of the evening fantasizing about getting out, about walking out on the grass and dirt beyond the fence. Of getting on a bus and going up north where my brother lived.

From there I would go up to Canada, maybe Alaska, and get lost somewhere in the wilderness where they wouldn't come hunting for me.

It was a dream I'd had since entering Aurora. A futile and useless dream, but I nurtured it day by day, hour by hour.

I could close my eyes and suddenly be transported to a glassy river, surrounded by mountains of pure white, and air so fresh and cold it could stop your lungs; an eagle would scream as it dropped from the sky to grab its prey.

But my eyes opened; the dream was gone.

In its place, the dull green of the walls, the smell of alcohol and urine, the sounds of Cap and Eddie screeching from their restraints two doors down, the small slit of window with the bright lights of the Yard on all night.

Only Joe kept me warm at night, and the smell of his hair as he scrunched in bed, snoring lightly beside me, kept alive any spirit that threatened to die inside me.

I had never been interested in men on the Outside, but in Aurora, it had never seemed homosexual between us.

It was survival.

When you are in that kind of environment, you seek warmth and human affection if you are at all sane. Even if sanity is just a frayed thread.

Even the sociopaths sought human warmth; even they, it is supposed, want to be loved.

I knew that Joe would one day kill me if I said the wrong thing to him, or if I wasn't generous in nature toward him. He had spent his life killing for those reasons.

Still, I took the risk because he was so warm and comfortable, and sometimes, at night, that's all you need.

The next morning I sought Hype out and plunked myself right down next to him.

"Why me?"

* * *

He didn't look up from his plate.

"Why not you?"

He had that stoned look of one who could see the invisible world. His smile was cocked, like a gun's trigger.

"Why not Doer, the compassionate? Doer, the one who serves? Why not you?"

"No," I said. "It could be any one of these guys. I've only been here four months. We don't know each other."

"I know everybody. I am infinite, I contain multitudes. I know all. Nothing is beyond me. I see the you within you. Besides, I told you, you don't pretend."

"Huh?"

"You don't pretend. You face things. That's important. It won't work if you live in your own little world, like most of these boys. You've got the talent."

"Yeah, the talent," I said, finally deciding the old fart was as loony as the rest.

"I saw what you did," he said.

As he spoke, I could feel my heart freeze. In the tone of his voice, the smoothness of old whiskey.

"I saw how you took the gun and killed your son first. One bullet to the back of the skull, and then another to his ear, just to make sure. Then your daughter, running through the house, trying to get away from you. She was actually the hardest, because she was screaming so much and moving so fast. You're not a good shot. It took you three bullets to bring her down."

"Just shut up," I said.

"Your wife was easy. She parked out front, and came in the side door, at the kitchen. She didn't know the kids were dead. All she knew was her husband was under a lot of pressure and she had to somehow make things right. She had groceries. She was going to cook dinner. While she was putting the wine in the fridge, you shot her and she died quickly. And then," Hype shook his head. "Then, you took the dog out, too. Who would take care of it, right? With everybody dead, who would take care of the dog?"

I said nothing.

"Who would take care of the dog?" he repeated. "You had no choice but to take it out, too. You loved that dog. It probably was as hard for you to pull the trigger on that dog as it was to pull it on your son. Maybe harder."

I said nothing. I thought nothing. My mind was red paint across black night. His words meant nothing to me.

He patted me on the back as my father had before the trial.

"It's all right. It's over. It wasn't anything anyone blames you for."

I began weeping; he rubbed his hand along my back and whispered words of comfort to me.

"It wasn't like that," I managed to say, drying my tears.

Although we had been left alone, I looked across the cafeteria and felt that all the others watched us.

Watched *me*, anyway.

But they didn't; they were preoccupied with their meals.

"It was…" I stumbled over words in my mind.

"Take your time," he said.

I wiped my face with filthy hands. I felt so dirty. I just wanted to be clean. I fought the urge to rise up and go find a shower.

"I wanted it to be me."

"But you wanted to live, too. You killed your family, and then suddenly—"

"*Suddenly*," I repeated.

"Suddenly, your life came back into focus. You couldn't kill yourself. You had to go through all of them before you found that out. Life's like that," he said. "The bad thing is, they're all dead. You did it. You're a murderer. But you're not like these others. It wasn't some genetic defect or some lack of conscience. Conscience is important. You couldn't kill yourself. That's important. I don't want to get some fellow out who's going to end up killing himself. You need to be part of something larger than yourself. You need God. Tell me, boy: How do you live with yourself?"

I couldn't look him in the eye. I was trying to think up a lie to tell him. He reached out and took my chin in his hand. He forced me to look at him.

I remembered a warning: he milks you with those eyes.

"I don't know how," I said, truthfully. "I wake up every morning and I think I am the worst human being in existence."

"Yes," he said. "You are. But here's the grace of Aurora. You're it. You will get out. You will live with what you did. You will not kill yourself or commit any further atrocities."

He let go of my chin and rose from the table. "You love your friend?"

"Joe?"

"That's right." He nodded. "Joe."

'Two guys can't love each other," I said. "It's just for now. It's surviving. It's barely even sexual."

"Ah." He nodded slowly. "That's good. It would be hell if you got out and you loved him and he was here. You must be careful around him, though. He is pretty and warm. But he has the face of Judas. He will never truly love anyone. Now, you, you will love again. A man, perhaps. Or a woman. But not our friend Joe. You know what he did to the last man he shared his bed with? He ever tell you?"

"No."

"Ask him," Hype said.

He walked away. From the back, he didn't seem old. He had a young way of walking.

I believed in him.

* * *

"Tonight. Late," Hype said to me later on, during our recreational time. "Two-thirty. You must first shower. You must be clean. I will not tolerate filth. Then wait. I will be there. If your friend makes trouble, stop him any way you can."

5

Joe could be possessive, but not in the expected way.

He wasn't jealous of other men or women. He simply wanted to own me all the time.

He wanted me to shower with him, to sit with him, to go to the cafeteria with him.

Our relationship seemed simple to me: we had met about the third week in, when he caught me masturbating in the bathroom.

He joined in, and this led to some necking, which led to a chilly week or so afterward when I felt strange from all that.

Then I got a letter from my mother in which she severed all connections with me, followed by one from my father and sister.

I spent two days in bed staring at the wall.

Joe came and took care of me until I could eat and stand and laugh again.

By that time, we were tight.

I had been at Aurora for less than two months before I realized I could not disentangle myself from Joe without being murdered or tortured – it was a Joe thing.

I didn't feel threatened, however. I'd grown fond of his occasional groping and nightly sleepovers.

In a way, it was like being a child again, with a best friend, with a mother and lover and buddy all rolled up into one person.

That night, when I rose from my bed at two a.m., Joe immediately woke up.

"Doer?" he asked.

"The can." I nodded toward the hallway.

Because Joe and I weren't in the truly dangerous category, we and a few others were given free rein of our hallway at night. Knowing, of course, that the Night Shift Bitch was on duty at the end of the hall.

"I'll go, too," Joe whispered, rising. He drew his briefs up. He had the endearing habit of leaving them down around his ankles in postcoital negligence.

I tapped him on the chest, shaking my head.

"Doer," he said, "I got to go, too."

The two of us quietly went into the hall.

In the bathroom, he said, "I know what's going on."

* * *

He leaned against the shiny tile wall. "It's Hype. Word went around. This is the night. Are you really going?"

I nodded, not wanting to lie. He had been sweet to me. I cared a great deal for him. I would be sad without him, for a time.

"I'll miss you, Joe. I really will."

"I could kill you for this."

"I know. But we're okay, buddy? You and me?"

"If you leave I'll be lonely. Maybe it's love, who knows?" He laughed, as if making fun of himself. "Maybe I love you. That's a good one."

"No you don't."

I imagined then that Joe was fairly incapable of something so morally developed as love, not because of his sexual leanings, but because of his pathology.

"Don't go," he said.

"For all I know, Hype is full of shit"

"He's not. I know things. I've seen him do this before. He gets people out. But don't go, Doer. Getting out's not so terrific."

"I want freedom," I said. "Plain and simple."

"I want you." Joe seemed to be getting a little testy.

"Now, come on, we're friends, you and me," I said, leaning forward to give him a friendly hug. "You're my buddy."

I didn't see the knife right away.

All I saw was something shiny, which caught the nearly-burnt-out light of the bathroom.

It didn't hurt going in — that was more a shock, like hearing an alarm clock at five a.m. waking you from a sound sleep.

Coming out, it hurt like a motherfucker.

He pressed his hand against the wound near my chest. "You can't leave me."

"Don't kill me, Joe. I won't leave you, I promise. You can come too." I gasped although I wasn't sure if the words in my mind formed from my lips or if I just imagined I said them as I slid downward.

He caught me in his arms and brought me down to cold tile.

I felt light-headed. The burning pain quickly turned to a frozen numbness.

I coughed, and wheezed, "get help, Joe. Please."

Joe pressed his sweaty body against mine.

Had he drawn his underwear down? I could feel his flesh against mine.

He murmured, a moan followed by softly whispered words that I couldn't make out.

I began to see brief tiny explosions of light and dark, as my vision faded.

Joe kissed the wound where he'd stabbed me, as blood pulsed from it.

"I love you this much," he said.

6

I awoke in the infirmary three days later, barely able to see through a cloud of painkillers.

I stared up at the ceiling until its small square acoustic tiles came into focus.

When I was better, months later, I went looking for Hype in the yard.

* * *

"I tried to make it," I said.

He seemed to look through me.

"You know what he did to me," I said. "Please, I want to get out. I have to get out."

After several minutes, Hype said, "Love transformed into fear. It's the human story. The last man Joe befriended was named Frank. He grew up in Compton. A good kid. He tore off another man's genitals with his bare hands and wore them around his neck.

"His only murder. Sweet kid. Twenty-two. Probably he was headed for release within a year or two. He had an A-plus evaluation. A little morbid. Used to draw pictures of beheadings. Joe latched on to him, too. Took care of him. Bathed him. Serviced him. Loved him, if you will. Then rumor went around that Frank was getting some from one of the psych techs. Totally fabricated, of course. Frank was taking a shower. Joe knocked him on the head. Strapped him to the bed, spread-eagled.

"Don't ask me how, but he'd gotten a hold of a drill—the old kind, you know, you turn manually and it spins. He made openings in Frank. First in his throat to keep him from screaming. Then the rest of him. Each opening…"

"I know," I said, remembering the pain under my arm. Then something occurred to me. "Where did he get the knife?"

Hype made a face, like he'd chewed something sour.

"The knife," I repeated. "And the drill, too. Everything's locked up tight. You're supposed to be God or something, so you tell me."

Without changing his expression, Hype said, "Joe gets out."

The enormity of this revelation didn't completely hit me. "From here?"

Hype nodded. "It's not something I'm proud of. I can open the door for about three hours, if I use up all my energy. Joe knows it. He was the first one I took out. But he didn't want to stay out. He only wanted out to get his toys. Then he wanted back. He's the only one who manages to get back. Why he wants to, I couldn't say."

For the first time ever, I watched worry furrow the old man's brow. He placed his hand against his forehead. A small blue vein pulsed there, beneath his pale skin's surface.

"I created the world, but it's not perfect."

"*Joe* knows how to get *out*?"

"I didn't say that. I can get it open. I just can't keep him from going back and forth. It something he does what nobody else seems able to do. And then the door closes again."

I wasn't sure how to pose my next question, because there was a mystery to this place where men got out. I had figured it to be down in the old underground, where Hype would know the route of the labyrinthine tunnels. "Where does *it* go?"

"That," Hype sighed, "I can't tell you, having never been through it. I just know it takes you out."

7

Back in my own bed that night, trying to sleep, I felt Joe's hand on my shoulder. He slipped swiftly between the covers to cradle my body against his.

"Doer," he said. "I missed you."

"Get off me." I tried to shrug him away. He was burning with some fever. A few drops of his sweat touched the back of my neck.

"No." He tucked himself in closer to me. I could feel his warm breath on my neck. "I want you."

"Not after what you did."

He said nothing more with words. His mouth opened against my neck, and I felt his tongue heat my sore muscles. All his language came through his throat and mouth, and I let him. I hated him, but I let him. Afterward, I whispered, "I want out."

"No, you don't."

"Yeah, I do. I don't care if you stab me again. I want out. You going to get me out?"

I waited a long time for his answer, then fell asleep.

I was still waiting for his answer a week later.

8

I cornered him in the shower, placing my hands on either side of him. I could encompass his body within my arms. I stared straight into his eyes.

"I want out."

He curled his upper lip; I thought he would answer, but first, he spat in my face.

"I saved you. You don't even care. Out is not where you want to be. In here's the only safe place. You get fed, you got a bed."

He leaned closer to me. "You have someone who loves you."

I was prepared this time. I brought my fist against his face and smashed him as hard as I could. His head lolled to the side, and I heard a sharp crack as his skull hit the tile wall. When he turned to face me again, there was blood at the corner of his lips. A smile grew from the blood.

"Okay," Joe said. "You want out. It can be arranged."

"Good. Next time, I kill you."

"Yeah." He nodded.

As I left the shower room, I glanced back at him for a second. He stood under the shower head, water streaming down—it almost looked like tears as the water streamed in rivulets across his face, taking with it the blood at his lips.

9

An hour later, Hype found me out by the crude baseball diamond we'd drawn in the Yard under the shade of several oak trees that grew just beyond the high fence.

"Your lover told me we're moving up the schedule. Shouldn't do this but once every few years. You should've gotten out that night. Joe shouldn't have stopped you. Any idea why he did?"

I kicked at home plate, a drawing in the dirt. Aurora was a funny place that way — because of things being considered dangerous around the inmates, even home plate had to be just a drawing and not the real thing. The real things here were the fences and the factory-like buildings.

"No," I said. "Maybe he's in love with me and doesn't want to lose me. I don't care. He can go to hell as far as I'm concerned."

"I once tried to get out all by myself," Hype said, ignoring me. "It was back in the early fifties. I was just a kid. Me and my buddies. I tried to get out, but back then there was only one way — a coffin. Not a happy system. I didn't know then that I'd rather be in here than out there."

"Make sense, old man," I said, frustrated. I wanted to kick him. The thought of spending another night in this place with Joe on top of me wasn't my idea of living.

"A little patience goes a long way, Doer," he said. It felt like a commandment.

He continued. "Then they started doing those tests — bombs and all kinds of things, twenty, thirty miles away. Some closer, they said. Some this side of the mountain.

"We lived below back then. Me and Skimp and Ralph. Others, too, but these were my tribe. We were shell-shocked and crazy, and we were put in with the paranoid schizophrenics and sociopaths and alcoholics — all of us together. Some restrained to a wall, some bound up in straitjackets. Some of us roaming free in the subterranean hallways. Skimp, he thought he was still on a submarine. He really did. But I knew where we were — in the farthest ring of hell.

"And then, one morning, around three a.m., I heard Skimp whimpering from his bunk. I go over there, because he had nightmares a lot. I usually woke him up and told him a story so he could fall back to sleep.

"Only, Skimp was barely there. His flesh had melted like cheese on a hot plate, until it was hard to tell where the sheets left off and Skimp began. He was making a noise through his nostrils. It was like someone snoring, only he was trying to scream.

"Others, too, crying out, and then I felt it — like my blood was spinning around. I heard since that it was like we got stuck in a microwave. The entire place seemed to shimmer, and I knew to cover my eyes. I had learned a little bit about these tests, and I knew that moist parts of the body were the most vulnerable. That's why insects aren't very affected by it — they've got exoskeletons. All their softs parts are on their insides. I felt drunk and happy, too, even while my mouth opened to scream, and I went to my hiding place, covering myself with blankets. I crawled as far back into my hiding place as I could go, and then I saw some broken concrete and started scraping at it. I managed to push my way through it, farther, into darkness. But I got away from the noise and the heat.

"Later, I heard that it was some test that had leaked out. Some underground nuclear testing. We were all exposed, those who survived. Never saw Skimp or Ralph again. I was told they were transferred. Back in those days, no one investigated anyone or anything. I knew they'd died, and I knew how they'd died. There were times I wished I'd died, too. Every day.

"That's when I learned about my divinity. It was like Christ climbing the cross—he may or may not have been God before he climbed onto that cross, but you know for sure he was God once he was up there. I wasn't God before that day, but afterward, I was."

Hype was a terrific storyteller, and while I was in awe of that ability, I stared at him as if he were the most insane man on the face of the earth.

"So I found a way out," he concluded.

"If that's true, how come you don't get out?"

"It's my fate. Others can go through, but I must stay. It's my duty. Trust me, you think God likes to be on Earth? It's as much an asylum out there as it is in here."

I was beginning to think that all of this talk about going through and getting out was an elaborate joke for which the only punch line would be my disappointment. I decided to hell with it all: The old man could not get me out no matter how terrific his stories were. I was going to spend the rest of my life with Joe pawing me.

I went to bed early, hoping to find some escape in dreams.

I awoke that night, a flashlight in my face.

10

Joe said, "Get up. This is what you want, right?"

His voice was calm, not the usual nocturnal passionate whisper of the Joe who caressed me. He hadn't touched me at all. I was somewhat relieved.

"Huh?" I asked. "What's going on?"

"You want to get out? Let's go. You've got to take a shower first."

I felt his hand tug at my wrist.

"Get the hell up," he said.

* * *

The shower was cold.

I spread Ivory soap across my skin, rubbing it briskly under my arms, around my healing wound, down my stomach, thighs, backs of legs, between my toes. Joe watched me the whole time. His expression was constant: a stone statue without emotion.

"It doesn't have to end like this," I said. "I'm going to miss you."

"Shut up," he said. "I don't like liars."

After I toweled off, he led me, naked, down the dimly lit hall.

The alarm was usually on at the double doors at the end of the hall, but its light was shut off.

Joe pushed the door open, guiding me along. The place seemed dead.

Hearing the sound of footsteps in the next ward, he covered my mouth with his hand and drew me quickly into an inmate's room.

Then, a few minutes later, we continued on to the cafeteria.

He had a key to the kitchen; he unlocked its door.

I followed him through the dark kitchen, careful to avoid bumping into the great metal counters and shelves.

Finally, he unlocked another door at the rear of the kitchen.

This led to a narrow hallway.

At the end of the hallway, another door, which was open.

Hype stood there, frozen in the flashlight beam.

11

———◦•◦———

"Hey," I said.

Hype put a finger to his lips. He wore a bathrobe that seemed shiny purple in the light.

He turned, going ahead of us, with Joe behind me. I followed the old man down the stone steps.

We entered the old Aurora, the one that stretched for miles beneath the above ground Aurora. We walked single file down more narrow corridors, the sound of dripping water all around.

At one point, I felt something brush my feet— a large insect, perhaps, or a mouse. The place smelled of wet moss, and carried its own humidity, stronger than what existed in the upper world.

For a while it did seem that Hype had been right:

This was the deepest ring of hell.

But I'm getting out, I thought. I'll go through any sewer that man has invented to get out. To go through. To be done with all this.

Joe rested his hand on my shoulder for a brief moment. He whispered in my ear, "You don't have to do this. I was wrong. I love you. Don't get out."

I stopped, feeling his sweet breath on my neck. Even though I had been in Aurora only a little over four months, I had begun getting used to it. If I stayed longer, I would become part of it, and the outside world would be alien and terrifying to me. I saw it in other men, including Joe. This was the only world of importance to them.

"Why the change?" I asked.

"You don't want to go through. I want you here with me."

"No, thanks." I put all the venom I could into those two words. I added, "And by the way, Joe, if I had a gun I'd shoot your balls off for what you did to me."

"You don't understand." He shook his head like a hurt little boy.

Hype was already several steps ahead. I caught up with him while Joe lagged behind.

"I'm going out through that hiding place you talked about," I guessed.

"No," he said. When he got to a cell, he led me through the open doorway.

A feeble light emanated within the room—a yellowish-green light, as if glow-worms had been swiped along the walls until their phosphorescence remained.

It was your basic large tank, looking as if it had been compromised by several earthquakes over the past few years.

Joe entered behind me. "This is where Hype and his friends lived. This is where it happened."

He waved the flashlight beam across the green light.

I shivered, because for a moment I felt as if the ghosts of those men were still here, trapped in the old Aurora.

"Tell him, Hype. Tell him."

Hype wandered the room, as if measuring the paces.

"Ralph had this area. He had his papers and books — he was always a big reader. Skimp was over there," he pointed to the opposite side of the cell, "his submarine deck."

"Tell him the whole thing," Joe said.

In the green light of the room, as I glanced back at Joe, I saw that he had a revolver in his right hand.

"Tell him," he repeated.

"Where the hell did you get that?" I pointed to the gun.

"You can't ever go back," Hype said. "Once you're out, you can never go back. I won't let you back. Understood?"

I nodded. As if I was ever going to want to return to Aurora.

"Tell him," Joe said to Hype. This time he pointed the gun at Hype.

Then, to me, he said, "The gun was down here. I get all my weapons here. We get all kinds of things down here. Hype is God, remember? He creates all things."

'To hell with this," I said, figuring this bad make believe had gone too far. "You can't get me out, can you?"

Hype nodded. "Yes, I can. I am God, Joe. Those underground tests, they made me God. They were my cross. I'm the only survivor. The orderlies, the doctors, the patients, I'm the only one. That's when I became God."

"You want to get out, right?" Joe snarled at me. "Right?" He waved the gun for me to move over to the far wall.

Hype turned, dropping his robe.

Beneath it he was naked, the skin of his back like a long festering sore.

The imprint of hundreds of stitches all along his spine, across the back of his rib cage.

To the right of this, a fist-sized cavity just above his left thigh.

"Tell him," Joe said.

The old man began speaking, as if he couldn't confess this to my face.

"Inside me is the door. The tunnel, Joe. To get through, you've got to enter me."

The must vulgar aspect of this hit me, and I groaned in revulsion.

Joe laughed. "Not what you think, Doer. Not like what you like to do to me. Or vice versa. His skin changed after the tests. Down here, it changes again. Look—it's like a river, look!"

At first I didn't know what he was pointing at—his finger tapped against Hype's wrinkled back.

Then, before I noticed any change, I felt something deep in my gut.

A tightening.

A terrible physical coiling within me, as if my body knew what was happening before my brain did.

I watched in horror as the old man's skin rippled along the spine. A slit broke open from one of the ancient wounds. It widened, gaping.

Joe came closer, shining his flashlight into its crimson-spattered entry.

It was like a red velvet curtain, moist, undulating. A smell like a dead animal from within.

The scent, too, of fresh meat,

Joe pressed the gun against my head. "Go through."

My first instinct was to resist.

Seconds later, Joe shot a bullet into the old man's wound, and it expanded further like the mouth of a baby bird as it waits for its feeding.

Joe kissed my shoulder. "Goodbye, Doer."

He pressed the gun to my head.

The old man's back no longer seemed to be there; now it was a doorway, a tunnel toward some green light at the end of a long red road.

His body had stretched its flesh out like a skinned beast, an animal-hide doorway.

With the gun against my head, Joe shoved me forward, into it.

I pushed my way through the slick red mass and followed the green light of atomic waste.

Once inside, the walls of crimson pushed me with a peristaltic motion deeper, against my will.

Tiny hooks of his bones caught the edge of my flesh, tugging backward while I was pressed into the opening.

12

We are all in here, all the others who got out through him.

Only, "out" didn't mean out of Aurora, not officially. We're out of our skins, drawn into that infested old man.

When I held the reins of him for an afternoon, I got him to go down and bribe the psych tech on duty.

I pulled up both of their files, Joe's and Hype's.

Joe was a murderer who had a penchant for cutting wounds in people and screwing the wounds. This was no surprise to me. Joe was a sick fuck. I knew it. Everyone who's ever been with him knows it.

Hype was a guy who had been exposed to large amounts of radiation in the fifties. He had a couple of problems, one physical and one mental. The physical one I am well aware of, for the little bag rests at the base of my stomach, to the side and back. Because of health problems as a result of the radiation, he'd had a colostomy about twenty years back.

The mental problems were also apparent to me once I got out, once I got through.

He suffered from a growing case of multiple personality disorder.

I pulled my file up, too, and it listed:

Escaped.

I had a good laugh with Joe over these files.

Then God took over, and I had to go back down into the moist tissues of heaven and wait until it was my turn again.

* * *

There are prisons within prisons, and skins within skins. You can't always see who someone is just by looking in his eyes.

Sometimes, others are there.

Sometimes, *God* is there.

"I am infinite," the old man said. "I contain multitudes."

ABOUT THE AUTHOR

Douglas Clegg is the *New York Times* bestselling and award-winning author of *Neverland*, *The Priest of Blood*, *Afterlife*, and *The Hour Before Dark*, among many other novels, novellas and stories. His short story collection, *The Machinery of Night*, won a Shocker Award, and his first collection, *The Nightmare Chronicles*, won both the Bram Stoker Award and the International Horror Guild Award. His work has been published by Simon & Schuster, Penguin/Berkley, Signet, Dorchester, Bantam Dell Doubleday, Cemetery Dance Publications, Subterranean Press, Alkemara Press, and others.

A pioneer in the ebook world, his novel *Naomi* made international news when it was launched as the world's first ebook serial in early 1999 and was called "the first major work of fiction to originate in cyberspace" by *Publisher's Weekly*, covered in *Time* magazine, *Business Week*, *Business 2.0*, *BBC Radio*, *NPR*, *USA Today* and more; his book *Purity* was the first to go onto a mobile phone in the U.S. in early 2001.

He is married, and lives and writes in New England.

To find the author's other novels, novellas, stories and collections, be sure to visit his website:

DouglasClegg.com